P9-ASF-130

Ripley's Believe It or Not!®

Developed and produced by Ripley Publishing Ltd

This edition published and distributed by:

Mason Crest
450 Parkway Drive, Suite D, Broomall, PA 19008
www.masoncrest.com

Printed and bound in the United States of America

First printing
9 8 7 6 5 4 3 2 1

Ripley's Believe It or Not!
Bizarre World
ISBN: 978-1-4222-3140-1 (hardback)
Ripley's Believe It or Not!—Complete 8 Title Series
ISBN: 978-1-4222-3138-8

Cataloging-in-Publication Data is on file with the Library of Congress

PUBLISHER'S NOTE
While every effort has been made to verify the accuracy of the entries in this book, the Publishers cannot be held responsible for any errors contained in the work. They would be glad to receive any information from readers.

WARNING
Some of the stunts and activities in this book are undertaken by experts and should not be attempted by anyone without adequate training and supervision.

Ripley's Believe It or Not!®

Dare To Look

BIZARRE WORLD

www.MasonCrest.com

BIZARRE WORLD

Amazing places. Open up to find some truly staggering stories. Read about the world beneath Europe's largest glacier, the ugly face contest, and the man who was stuck inside a frozen car for two months!

Two young goats spent two days stuck on the narrow 6-in-wide (15-cm) ledge of a railway bridge near Roundup, Montana...

DRESSING THE DEAD

As a way to demonstrate their love for the deceased, family members in the Toraja district of Indonesia exhume their ancestors' mummified bodies every three years and dress them in new clothes. As part of the strange ritual, called Ma'nene, the smartly attired dead are then taken for a walk around their local village.

The local people attach great importance to death and believe that family members are still with them, even if they died hundreds of years ago. Lavish funerals often take place months after death, by which time the corpses have been infused with preservatives so that they remain in good condition for centuries to come.

Villagers bind cloth rolls that contain their relatives.

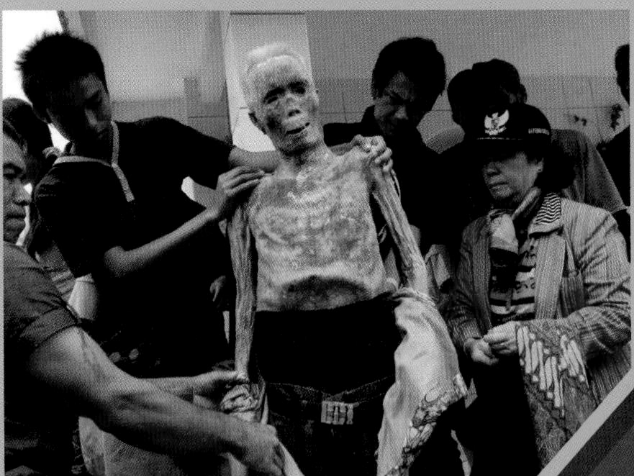

The deceased relative is dressed in a new set of clothes every three years.

Family members carry the coffin that contains their preserved relative dressed in new clothes.

The wealthiest people are usually buried in stone graves carved out of cliffs, while others are buried in caves. Their coffin contains possessions that the deceased will need in the afterlife. Coffins of babies or children are often hung from ropes on a cliff face or from a tree. These hanging graves last for years until the ropes rot and the coffin falls to the ground. Ma'nene takes place over a three-day period, usually in August. The coffins are lifted from their tombs and stored in a grave house at the heart of the ceremony.

Family members parade their relative around the village.

YOSEMITE FIREFALL

At 9 p.m. almost every summer night for 96 years, burning hot embers from wood fires were dropped 3,000 ft (900 m) from the top of Glacier Point in California's Yosemite National Park to the valley below in what looked from a distance like a glowing waterfall. The Yosemite Firefall, as it was known, was performed as a tourist attraction by several generations of the owners of the Glacier Point Hotel who would use long-handled metal implements to push the fire embers off the cliff evenly so as to simulate a steady flow. The spectacle was finally banned in 1968 and ironically the hotel burned down the following year.

CARRIAGE HOME A bungalow in Cornwall, England, is built around a 130-year-old railway carriage. The bedrooms in Jim Higgins's home are located in the restored carriage dating from 1882.

FISH RICH Lake Malawi, Africa's third largest lake, has an estimated 1,000 species of fish—more than every lake in North America combined.

STORMY DAY In a single day—June 28, 2012—the U.K. was hit by a record 110,000 lightning bolts, with more than 200 strikes recorded every minute at the height of the storms. This was 40 times higher than an average lightning storm and represented the equivalent of four months' worth of strikes in one day.

ICE SHOCK A huge block of ice fell from the sky and crashed through the roof of Brentwood Cathedral in Essex, England, during Sunday service, leaving members of the congregation trembling with shock. The ice is believed to have fallen from an airplane.

WOMEN DIVERS The fishing divers of Jeju Island, South Korea, are all women, a tradition that dates back hundreds of years. The average age of the 5,000 or so divers is 50, but some are over 80 years old. The practice began when a loophole in the law allowed women to sell their catch tax-free, while men were heavily penalized.

HOT RAIN The hottest rain ever recorded—115°F (46°C)—fell during a desert thunderstorm at Needles, California, on August 13, 2012. Owing to the low humidity, most of the rain evaporated before it hit the ground.

RED CITY Streets, sidewalks, and open spaces in the Chinese city of Foshan were covered in red clay in July 2012 after a typhoon washed the clay down from nearby mountains. Even when the floodwaters subsided, a red clay residue coated the ground and lower levels of buildings.

NEAR MISS On February 29, 2012, a tornado came within 40 ft (12 m) of the Ripley's Believe It or Not! Odditorium in Branson, Missouri—a building deliberately designed to look like it has been hit by an earthquake! The 1,200-ft-wide (366-m) tornado tore the roof from the motel next door but, believe it or not, spared the Odditorium, whose distinctive crumbling façade has made it one of the most photographed buildings in the world. It was erected in 1999 to commemorate the massive 1812 Missouri earthquake that made the Mississippi River run backward for three days and made church bells ring in Philadelphia, nearly 1,000 mi (1,600 km) away.

STONE FOREST

TOP TANKS▸ Water tanks on the roofs of residential buildings in Guiyang, China, are decorated as giant soccer balls. Local authorities thought that regular tanks would look too ugly, so they made them into a quirky feature of the neighborhood.

UNDERSEA ERUPTION▸ An underwater volcano erupted off the coast of New Zealand to create a mass of white, floating pumice that covered 10,000 sq mi (26,000 sq km) of the ocean—equivalent to the size of Belgium. The small, buoyant volcanic rocks were the size of golf balls and were formed when lava from the volcano came into contact with seawater.

▸A stone forest consisting of hundreds of razor-sharp vertical rocks—many up to 330 ft (100 m) high—covers a remote 230-sq-mi (595-sq-km) area of Madagascar. Known as the Tsingy, which translates as "where one cannot walk barefoot," the spectacular structure was formed by tropical rainfall eroding the limestone rock into spiked towers. Although it looks inhospitable, the landscape is home to a wide variety of animals, including 11 species of lemur.

FIREBALL FIGHT▸ To commemorate the mighty volcanic eruption of 1658 that forced the entire town to be evacuated, residents of Nejapa, El Salvador, have gathered every August 31 since 1922 to hurl fiery, gasoline-soaked rags at each other. Although there are no rules for the fireball fight, amazingly there have been few serious injuries.

EXTRA TIME▸ An extra second—known as a leap second—was added to time at midnight on June 30, 2012, because the Earth's rotation is slowing down.

STRANDED GOATS

▶ Two young goats spent two days stuck on the narrow, 6-in-wide (15-cm) ledge of a railway bridge 60 ft (18 m) above a highway near Roundup, Montana, before being rescued with a crane.

PRESS GANG▶ Under the "Barney Fife" ordinance, police officers in Johnson City, Tennessee, can draft citizens into law enforcement duties during illegal assemblies or riots—with refusal to serve being a crime.

FALLING FRUIT▶ An avalanche of more than 100 apples rained down like giant hailstones on a busy road in Coventry, England, on December 12, 2011, forcing stunned drivers to swerve and brake sharply. The fall of fruit is thought to have been caused by a freak mini tornado that lifted the green apples from a garden or orchard before dropping them in the city.

MINE HOST▶ Sweden's Sala silver mine has a hotel room located 508 ft (155 m) below ground. Access is by a mine lift shaft, and it took nearly ten years to carve out the room, which, because it is set in a warm air pocket, has a pleasant temperature of 64°F (18°C), compared to the chilly 36°F (2°C) elsewhere at the bottom of the mine.

MEN AT RISK▶ More than 80 percent of lightning strike victims are male. This is not because men are usually taller than women (lightning often strikes the tallest object), but because they tend to spend a greater amount of time outdoors.

ELECTION DAY▶ National elections in the United States always take place on a Tuesday owing to a law dating back to 1845 that gave people time to reach a voting station when traveling by horse. Tuesday was chosen because it did not clash with Sunday worship or market day, which was Wednesday in many towns.

INLAND BEACH

▸ Although it is 330 ft (100 m) from the sea in the middle of a green meadow, Playa de Gulpiyuri, near Llanes, Spain, is a flooded sinkhole that has its own beach and even its own waves. About 130 ft (40 m) long, it is affected by tides because the salt water of the Cantabrian Sea has carved a network of underground tunnels that constantly feed water to the beach from the Bay of Biscay. The gentle waves and crystal-clear water make the inland beach a popular tourist spot, but the water is colder than normal, having traveled underground.

INVISIBLE BRIDGE▸ Visitors can reach the historic Fort de Roovere in the Netherlands via a sunken bridge, which runs beneath the water level of the surrounding moat. As the water on either side comes right up to the edges of the bridge, the walkway is virtually invisible to the naked eye when viewed from a distance.

GLACIER THEFT▸ In January 2012, police in Chile arrested a man on suspicion of stealing five tons of ice from the Jorge Montt glacier near the Patagonian border to sell as designer ice cubes in bars and restaurants. Officers intercepted a refrigerated truck containing more than $5,000 worth of illicit ice.

SAFE HOUSE▸ In 2011, a home created from a nuclear missile silo in Saranac, New York State, went on sale for $1.76 million. It came complete with its own private airstrip and 15,000 sq ft (1,400 sq m) of underground space that was built to withstand tornadoes, hurricanes, and nuclear attacks.

CRASH LANDINGS▸ Thousands of migrating birds were killed or injured in Utah in December 2011 when stormy weather conditions caused them to mistake wet parking lots for ponds.

PIED PIPER▸ The German town of Hamelin was in need of a new Pied Piper in 2012 following a fresh invasion of rats. The rodents, attracted by people feeding birds, chewed through electrical cables, putting a local fountain out of order.

DRIVE-IN CHURCH▸ Reverend David Ray, a Presbyterian Church pastor in Texas, holds some of his church services in the style of drive-in movie theaters, with parishioners seated in their cars in a parking lot.

DO NOT DISTURB▸ The Mashco-Piro tribe, an isolated Amazon tribe in southeastern Peru, seeks to avoid contact with the outside world by firing tipless arrows as warning shots for tourists and park rangers to keep away.

FLOUR BOMBS▸ At the Els Enfarinats festival in Ibi, Spain, an event that dates back more than 200 years, revelers dressed in mock military uniforms pelt each other with flour and eggs.

DULL AND BORING▸ In 2012, the town of Boring, Oregon, voted to become a "sister community" to Dull, Scotland. Boring was named after William Boring, a local resident, and Dull is thought to come from the Pictish word for field.

SPIDER NIGHTMARE

Spiders from the town of Wagga Wagga, in New South Wales, Australia, spun some amazing webs while escaping floodwaters in March 2012.

As the waters rushed past the town, the spiders were forced to scuttle out of the way, climbing up trees and bushes, and spinning their webs as they went. The results were fields that looked like they were covered in snow, bushes that looked like giant cotton candy, and dogs that could play hide-and-seek from their owners for hours!

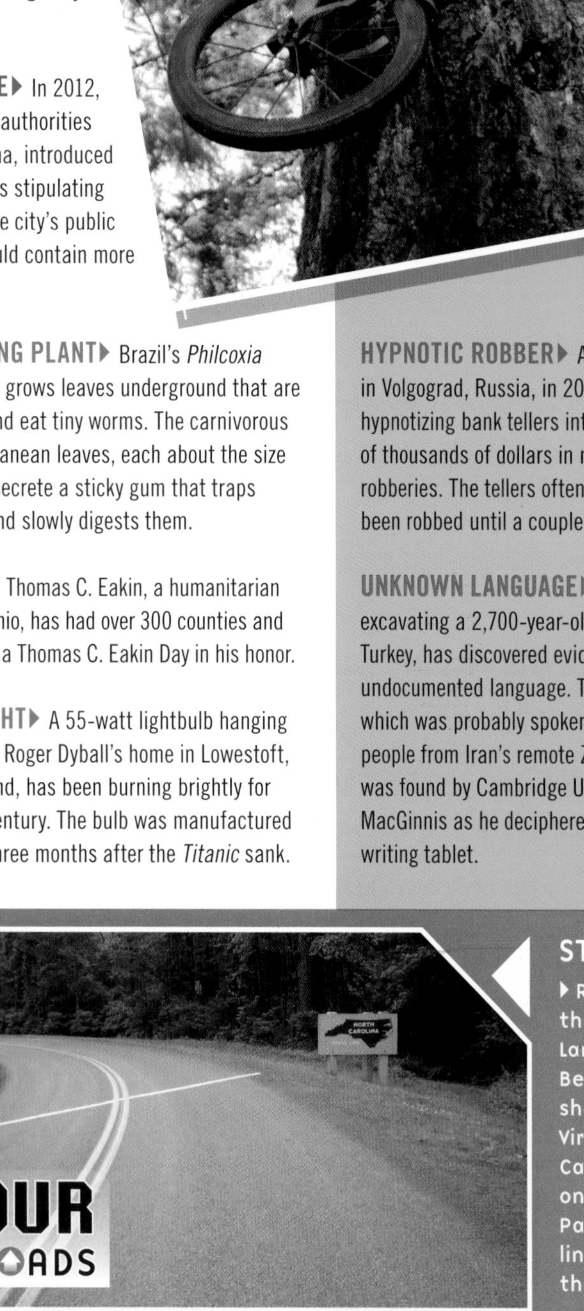

GREEDY TREE

▸ This tree on Vashon Island, Washington, has eaten a bicycle! The story behind the bizarre phenomenon has been the stuff of legend for years—even spawning a children's book—but recent new evidence suggests that the red bicycle was abandoned next to the tree by local boy Don Puz in 1954 and that the trunk subsequently grew around it. Even so that does not explain why the bicycle is more than 6 ft (1.8 m) above the ground. Maybe there is still a final part of the mystery waiting to be solved.

TSUNAMI BIKE ▸ A Harley-Davidson motorbike was washed up on the coast of British Columbia, Canada, in April 2012, having been swept into the sea by the Japanese tsunami 13 months earlier. The rusty bike with a Japanese license plate was found on Graham Island and was traced to an owner in Miyagi Prefecture, a region of Japan badly damaged by the tsunami.

NO-FLY ZONE ▸ In 2012, environmental authorities in Beijing, China, introduced new regulations stipulating that none of the city's public lavatories should contain more than two flies.

WORM-EATING PLANT ▸ Brazil's *Philcoxia minensis* plant grows leaves underground that are used to trap and eat tiny worms. The carnivorous plant's subterranean leaves, each about the size of a pinhead, secrete a sticky gum that traps roundworms and slowly digests them.

TOM'S DAY ▸ Thomas C. Eakin, a humanitarian from Aurora, Ohio, has had over 300 counties and cities proclaim a Thomas C. Eakin Day in his honor.

SHINING LIGHT ▸ A 55-watt lightbulb hanging in the porch of Roger Dyball's home in Lowestoft, Suffolk, England, has been burning brightly for more than a century. The bulb was manufactured in July 1912, three months after the *Titanic* sank.

HYPNOTIC ROBBER ▸ A woman was arrested in Volgograd, Russia, in 2009, on suspicion of hypnotizing bank tellers into handing over tens of thousands of dollars in more than 30 separate robberies. The tellers often did not realize they had been robbed until a couple of hours later.

UNKNOWN LANGUAGE ▸ A British archeologist excavating a 2,700-year-old palace in Tushan, Turkey, has discovered evidence of a previously undocumented language. The mystery language—which was probably spoken by a formerly unknown people from Iran's remote Zagros Mountains—was found by Cambridge University's Dr. John MacGinnis as he deciphered an ancient clay writing tablet.

HUMAN HAMSTERS ▸ A Ferris wheel in New Delhi, India, has no motors and is powered instead entirely by human muscle. The men hang from the inner bars of the wheel and use their weight to propel it around like human hamsters.

AEROBIC TREMOR ▸ A 10-minute tremor that caused hundreds of people to flee screaming from a high-rise building in Seoul, South Korea, on July 5, 2011, was caused by 17 middle-aged fitness fanatics enjoying a vigorous gym exercise workout on the 12th floor.

HARMS' WAY ▸ Virgil Harms has served as mayor of Paoli, Colorado, for more than 50 years, having never faced an opponent during an election.

DEATH RITUAL ▸ When a person dies among the Jarawa people of the Andaman Islands, relatives place the body beneath a tree where it sits until it is reduced to a skeleton. Then the members of the tribe tie the bones to their own bodies to bring luck while hunting pigs and fishing for turtles.

LUCKY VILLAGE ▸ Every French soldier to serve from the small village of Thierville in Normandy has come back alive in the country's last five wars—including World War I and World War II.

METEORITE TOWN ▸ The town of Manson, Iowa, sits on top of a 74-million-year-old meteorite crash site that disrupted the underlying rock so badly that it is nearly impossible to drill water wells in the area.

YOUR UPLOADS

STATE LINE

▸ Ripley's were sent this picture by Dick Larson of West Palm Beach, Florida, showing that the Virginia–North Carolina state line on the Blue Ridge Parkway is an actual line painted on the road!

GHOST SKULLS

Thirteen golden human skulls form a macabre religious shrine in Bangkok, Thailand, guarding the newly dead and preventing their souls from turning into malevolent ghosts.

The shrine was built more than 60 years ago by a volunteer ambulance company—and the skulls belonged to nameless ambulance patients who died while being transported to the hospital and whose bodies were never claimed. After having the corpses cremated, the company kept the skulls, cleaned them, covered them in gold paint and gold leaf, and later inserted small gold lamé cushions into the eye sockets. When the ambulance company eventually moved from its warehouse headquarters, it left the shrine behind, the skulls' spirits acting to safeguard the building.

As they originally belonged to dead paupers or unidentified "John Does," the skulls are seen as kindly benefactors, protecting the bodies of the deceased and comforting their spirits during the period between death and disposal of the body.

Local superstition states that the souls of the poor and the anonymous are particularly susceptible to ghostly interference and that unless a fresh corpse is cared for, the spirits of these downtrodden folk will linger and become infested with evil.

NOCTURNAL ORCHID▶ On New Britain Island, near Papua New Guinea, botanists have discovered the world's first night-flowering orchid. Of the 25,000 species of orchid, *Bulbophyllum nocturnum* is the only one with flowers that consistently open after dark and then close up in the morning.

LOST BALL▶ A soccer ball that was swept out to sea by the Japanese tsunami in March 2011 was found more than a year later on a beach on Alaska's Middleton Island over 3,000 mi (4,800 km) away and returned to its owner, 16-year-old Misaki Murakami.

CLAN CAMPBELL▶ When the town of Phil Campbell, Alabama, was hit by a tornado on April 27, 2011, men and women named Phil and Phyllis Campbell from all over the world raised nearly $35,000 for relief efforts.

SKY-HIGH▶ Opened on May 22, 2012, the Tokyo Sky Tree is the world's tallest free-standing tower. The steel structure weighs over 45,000 tons and houses a staircase of 2,523 steps. At 2,080 ft (634 m) tall, the Japanese landmark is nearly twice the height of the Eiffel Tower.

UNIQUE LAVA▶ Carbonatite lava, which is only about half the temperature of typical lava, flows freely with a viscosity similar to motor oil and can be found in only one place on Earth—Ol Doinyo Lengai, a volcano in Tanzania.

SIX STRIKES▶ Carl Mize, a University of Oklahoma utility employee, has miraculously survived six different lightning strikes. The odds of being struck by lightning just once in a lifetime are 5,000 to 1, which makes Mize a guy in several million.

MANHATTAN SOLSTICE▶ On two days of the year—the first occurring around the end of May and the second in the middle of July—the sun sets precisely in line with the street grid of Manhattan, New York City. The extraordinary phenomenon is known as "Manhattanhenge" (named after the solstice site of Stonehenge in the U.K.) or "the Manhattan Solstice."

DRY SNOW▶ A snowball cannot be made at the snow-covered South Pole. The snow there is too dry and powdery to clump together.

LAVA LAKE▶ The Democratic Republic of Congo's Mount Nyiragongo has one of the world's largest permanent lava lakes, with a huge 1,800°F (982°C) pool of molten rock often measuring 1,300 ft (396 m) deep and holding an estimated 282 million cubic ft (8 million cubic m) of lava.

WEIRD LAKE▶ Lake Untersee, which lies under a thick layer of ice in Antarctica, has water as alkaline as bleach and sediments that produce more methane than any other lake on Earth.

RED RIVER▶ On December 12, 2011, an industrial accident involving chemical dye caused the Jian River in Henan, China, to turn blood red.

ALGAE BLOOM▶ In July 2010, the Baltic Sea experienced a blue-green algae bloom covering an area of 145,500 sq mi (377,000 sq km)—larger than the size of Germany. It was triggered by a lack of wind, prolonged high temperatures, and fertilizers being washed into the sea from surrounding farmland.

LIVING DEAD▶ The seedpod of the ice plant, *Delosperma nakurense*, can open and close itself even after it has fallen from the plant and died.

TOXIC DUMP▶ The city of Orlando, Florida, pumped tens of thousands of gallons of molasses into the ground to clean up a toxic dump. The molasses was injected into the ground to break up the chemical that had contaminated the land.

MOSSY ISLAND▶ Buckeye Lake, Ohio, is home to an 11-acre (4.5-ha) floating island made of sphagnum moss covered in countless rare species, cranberry plants, and trees. The bog is a relic of the Ice Age.

LIPSTICK DAMAGE▶ The tomb of Irish writer Oscar Wilde in Paris, France, needed restoration in 2011 due to it being eaten away by lipstick from tourists kissing the monument.

PRESERVED FOREST▶ Scientists have discovered a huge 298-million-year-old forest buried intact beneath a coal mine near Wuda, Inner Mongolia, China. As the forest had been covered and preserved for all those centuries by volcanic ash, entire trees and plants were found exactly as they were at the time of the eruption.

GEL STORM▶ During a freak 20-second hail storm over Bournemouth, England, on January 26, 2012, when the sky turned a peculiar dark yellow, about 20 blue jellylike spheres, each the size of a marble, fell to the ground. Tests later showed them to be floristry hydrating gels, but nobody knows how they came to fall from the sky.

QUAKE SCALE▶ An 8.7 earthquake is about 23,000 times more powerful than a 5.8 earthquake. The release of energy in an earthquake multiplies by nearly 32 times with every whole number increase on the Richter scale.

VOLCANIC ERUPTIONS▶ At any one moment there are about 20 volcanoes actively erupting around the world. Of the 600 or so volcanoes that have erupted in history, about 10 percent erupt each year.

MANY TONGUES▶ There are more than 800 languages spoken on the island of New Guinea—about a third of the world's indigenous tongues—making it the most linguistically diverse place on Earth.

EXPLOSIVE HEAT▶ Scientists have created the hottest temperature ever seen on Earth—an incredible 10 trillion degrees Fahrenheit (5.5 trillion degrees Celcius), 250,000 times hotter than the Sun. The ultra-hot explosions, each of which lasted for less than one-billionth of a second, were created on a giant atom smasher at the Large Hadron Collider outside Geneva, Switzerland.

BACK TO LIFE▶ Russian scientists have successfully grown plants of *Silene stenophylla* from tissue material that had remained intact, frozen in the ground in Siberia, for 30,000 years.

TOWERING INFERNO

▸ *In September 2012, filmmaker Chris Tangey was scouting movie locations in Alice Springs, Australia, when he captured a fire tornado on camera. This rarely witnessed natural phenomenon occurs when flames on the ground are whipped into a whirlwind that can spiral as high as 1,000 ft (300 m) and last for more than an hour. Chris described the fire as sounding like a "fighter jet."*

CORPSE BRIDE

For more than 80 years, visitors from all over the world have been lured to a wedding gown shop in Chihuahua, Mexico, to study the spookily lifelike bridal mannequin in the window. According to legend, the mannequin is not really a model at all, but the perfectly preserved corpse of the previous owner's daughter.

Most are so captivated by the mesmerizing gaze of La Pascualita, as she is known, that they leave convinced that she is a mummy rather than a dummy. She was first installed in the window in 1930, but people soon realized that she bore an uncanny likeness to the store's owner at the time, Pascuala Esparza. They concluded that the apparent mannequin was really the embalmed body of Esparza's daughter who had died recently on her wedding day after being bitten by a black widow spider. Esparza denied the story, but the rumors persisted, and La Pascualita began to take on a life of her own. It is said that a love-struck French magician would arrive at night and bring her to life, taking her out on the town. Others say her eyes follow them around the store and that she changes positions during the night. One shop worker, Sonia Burciaga, who has to change the dummy's outfits twice a week, says: "Every time I go near Pascualita my hands break out in a sweat. Her hands are very realistic and she even has varicose veins on her legs. I believe she's a real person."

CHILLY CHURCH Residents of the German village of Mitterfirmiansreut built a church from snow and ice in December 2011, complete with a 62-ft-tall (19-m) tower. It held 200 people and was built to commemorate a similar snow church constructed there exactly 100 years earlier.

EGG ROULETTE At the Russian Egg Roulette World Championships, held in Lincolnshire, England, each competitor picks an egg from a box of six, five of which have been hard-boiled and one left raw. The eggs are then smashed against the competitors' heads, the losers being the ones left—literally—with egg on their face.

MR. CLEAN Don Aslett of Pocatello, Idaho, has opened the Museum of Clean, which features 6,000 vacuums, dust busters, rug beaters, and other items relating to the history of cleanliness. Among the artifacts are a horse-drawn vacuum cleaner dating back to 1902, an antique Amish footbath, and a 1,600-year-old bronze toothpick. The seats in the museum continue the theme, being fashioned out of garbage bins, a claw-foot bathtub, and a 1945 washing machine.

FLOUR BOMBS Every February in Galaxidi, Greece, dozens of people put on goggles, face masks, plastic suits, and cow bells to fight each other by hurling hundreds of small bags filled with a combined total of more than two tons of colored sticky baking flour. Lasting for several hours, the Flour War creates such a mess that houses and boats in the coastal town have to be covered in plastic.

RED LAKE

A lake in the Camargue area of southern France turned blood red in August 2012 as a result of its high salt concentration linked to the tiny brine shrimp that live in the lake. When the salt concentration in the lake is very high, the shrimp die and saline algae spread rapidly to give the water its unusual color.

LARGE PRINT

The parking garage at Kansas City Public Library, Missouri, is covered by a "shelf" of huge wooden book spines, each measuring 25 x 9 ft (7.6 x 2.7 m). Known as the "Community Bookshelf," the 22 titles, which include *The Lord of the Rings*, *Romeo and Juliet*, and *To Kill a Mockingbird*, were suggested by library users.

BOTTLE HOMES Twenty-five homes in Yelwa, Nigeria, are being built entirely from sand-filled, discarded plastic water bottles, placed on their side, one on top of the other, and bound together with mud. The recycled bottles serve as good insulation, and are both inexpensive and bullet-resistant. Each house uses around 7,800 bottles.

POWER OUTAGE Following the collapse of three electrical grids, a massive two-day power outage in India on July 30–31, 2012, affected more than 600 million people—about half the country's population.

KNIT WIT The Hotel Pelirocco in Brighton, England, has a room where everything is made from wool—including a vase of flowers, curtains, a toothbrush, a tube of toothpaste, and even the breakfast. Using 11 lb (5 kg) of wool, designer Kate Jenkins also knitted a bedspread from 100 different colors and crocheted covers for the phone, lampshade, teapot, and cup.

HIVE OF ACTIVITY

Collecting the precious honeycomb can take several hours. The harvesters use simple bamboo sticks.

The honeycomb is lowered to the ground in a handmade basket.

Continuing a tradition that dates back hundreds of years and has claimed many lives, the Rai people of Nepal make ladders out of braided bamboo to climb 250 ft (76 m) up a steep mountain cliff and harvest the prized honey of the world's largest bee, the Himalayan honey bee.

The harvesters light a fire at the base of the cliff to smoke the bees from their honeycombs and then, often under attack from up to 100,000 swarming bees, they retrieve the 5-ft-wide (1.5-m) honeycombs with long sticks in a delicate four-hour mission before lowering the booty to the ground.

The climbers wear no facial protection to guard against stings—their only safety precaution is to tie their feet to the homemade ladders to reduce the risk of a fall. Ironically, the red honey, which sells for five times the price of regular honey, is poisonous owing to a toxin in the pollen and nectar of the rhododendron plants used to make it. When consumed straight out of the honeycomb, it can result in stomach cramps and vomiting, so it is often used as a substitute for sugar and as an ingredient in pancakes. Despite its toxic properties, the honey remains sought-after, as it is believed to possess healing and relaxing powers.

A Rai honey harvester carrying a huge honeycomb.

RING ROAD

When an elderly couple in Wenling, China, refused to let their five-story house be demolished to make way for a new road, planners simply built the road around it. Luo Baogen and his wife lived in the last house standing, being circled by cars and trucks.

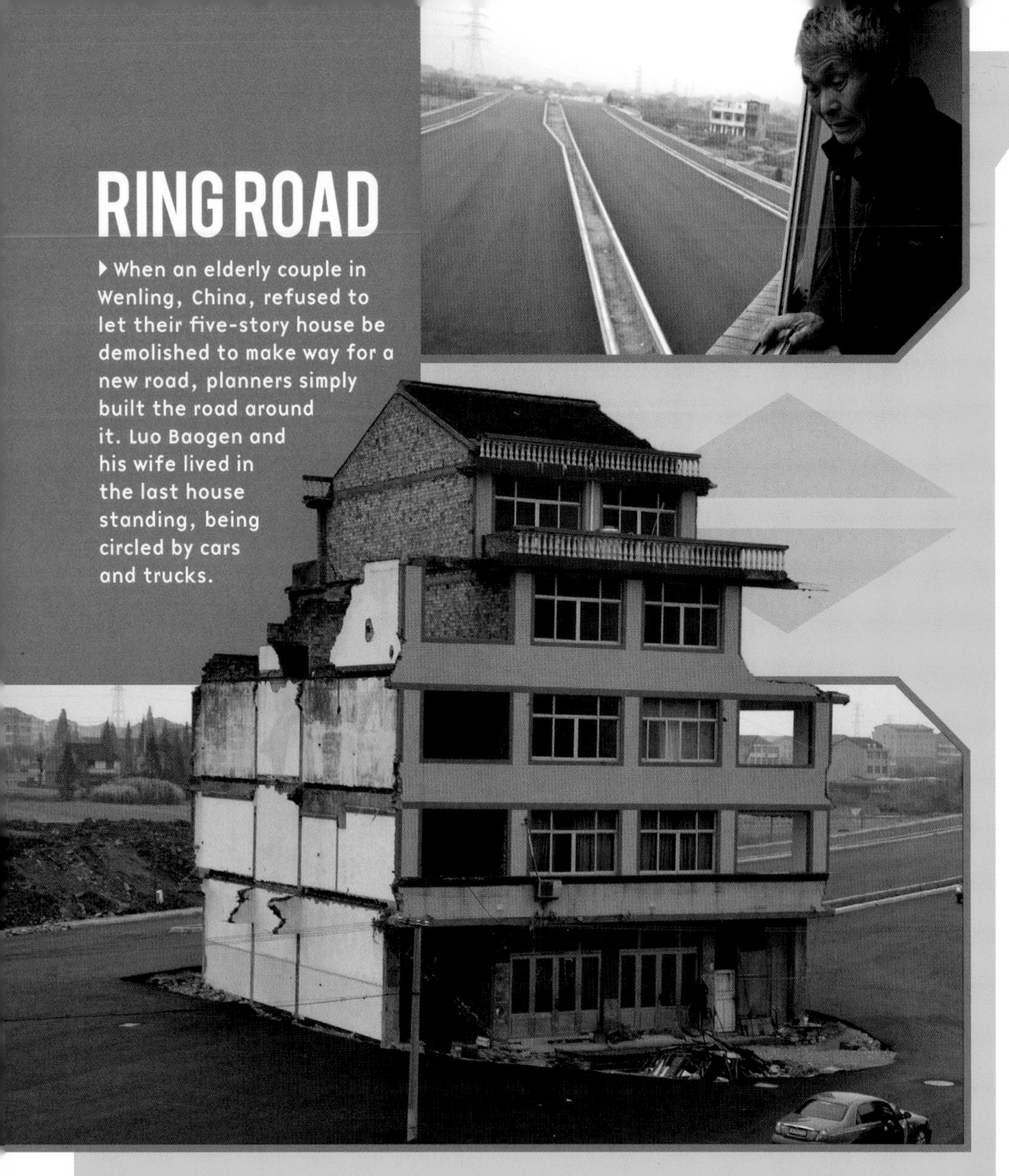

SILVER BULLION In 2012, a record haul of around 48 tons of silver bullion, worth around $44 million, was recovered from a World-War-II wreck 15,000 ft (4,570 m) deep in the Atlantic off the coast of Ireland. The 1,203 bars of silver were retrieved from the S.S. *Gairsoppa*, a British cargo ship that was sunk by a German torpedo in 1941.

FLYING ANGEL Italy's annual 12-day Venice Carnival begins with the "Flight of the Angel," where a young woman is suspended on a wire from a bell tower 330 ft (100 m) above St. Mark's Square and is gradually lowered to the ground.

ABOVE GROUND More than half of the London Underground's 250-mile (400-km) subway network is actually overground.

SCARY POOL The glass-bottomed swimming pool at the Holiday Inn hotel in Shanghai, China, partly hangs over a 24-story drop, giving swimmers a scary bird's-eye view of the street below. The 100 x 20 ft (30 x 6 m) cantilever pool is designed to make guests feel as if they are swimming in the sky.

IDENTICAL SHRUBS Every King's Lomatia, a shrub from Tasmania, is genetically identical. The plants never produce fruit or seeds and can only reproduce when a branch falls off and grows a root of its own.

DISAPPEARING SEA The Aral Sea—on the border of Kazakhstan and Uzbekistan—was once the fourth-largest inland lake in the world, covering 26,300 sq mi (68,000 sq km) with more than 1,500 islands dotted in its waters. However, after 50 years of water diversion, it is now mostly desert split into four lakes and has shrunk to one-tenth of its original size. In the 1950s, Muynak was located on the edge of the water; today it is a desert town more than 62 mi (100 km) from the sea. The disappearance of the Aral Sea has been blamed for local climate change, with summers becoming hotter and drier, and winters colder and longer.

HEAVY CLOUDS The water droplets in a medium-sized cumulus cloud weigh as much as 80 elephants. Large cumulonimbus clouds can be twice the height of Mount Everest.

BALL STORM Hundreds of tiny, yellow plastic balls fell from the sky over Dylis and Tony Scott's garden in Leicester, England, during a thunderstorm on August 19, 2012. Mysteriously, the lightweight balls, which may have been picked up many miles away by the wind and transported in the storm, were soon washed away by the rain.

CLOUD RIDERS A mysterious and rare meteorological phenomenon known as the morning glory cloud appears every fall above the small town of Burketown, Queensland, Australia. Each year, glider pilots convene to ride the tubular clouds, which can stretch for 620 mi (1,000 km), be as low as 330 ft (100 m) above ground, and move at speeds of 37 mph (60 km/h).

ECCENTRIC OLYMPICS As an alternative to the 2012 Olympics, London also staged the Chap Olympiad, a celebration of English eccentricity featuring events such as bicycle jousting, butler baiting, throwing a bowler hat into a fishing net, and ironing board surfing, where competitors are carried atop an ironing board while holding a cocktail that they must not spill.

SNAIL HOUSE A five-story family house in Sofia, Bulgaria, has been designed in the shape of a giant snail. The brightly colored snail house has horns on its head and butterflies on its back and took nearly ten years to build without a single straight wall or corner. The interior is equally quirky, with heating radiators in the form of a frog, a ladybug, and a pumpkin.

THERE ARE OVER 10 MILLION BRICKS IN THE EMPIRE STATE BUILDING.

DRIP... DRIP Ohio State University in Columbus, Ohio, has an international hall of fame dedicated to water drainage.

RECKLESS DRIVER A driver from Zurich, Switzerland, committed 15 traffic violations in just over ten minutes—including speeding, driving on the hard shoulder, running a set of red lights, and failing to stop for police.

BUBBLE HOTEL At the Bubble Hotel, set in the countryside outside Paris, France, guests sleep in inflatable rooms that have a transparent dome so that they can admire the wonders of nature.

ANCIENT LOVE Archeologists in Modena, Italy, have unearthed the skeletal remains of a Roman-era couple who have been holding hands for the past 1,500 years. The man and woman died around the late 5th century and were buried apparently looking longingly into each other's eyes.

REMOTE ACCESS

The 200 villagers of Yushan in Hubei Province, China, are completely cut off from the outside world except for a 3,300-ft-long (1,000-m) aerial ropeway stretched between two sheer cliffs. To go shopping, they must ride in a diesel-powered steel cage suspended precariously from cables 1,300 ft (400 m) above the valley floor. Before the cable link was built, the villagers had to walk for several days to reach the nearest village.

DEATH OF A PRESIDENT

On Friday, November 22, 1963, John Fitzgerald Kennedy, aged 46, the 35th President of the United States, was assassinated while traveling in a motorcade alongside his wife Jacqueline through the streets of downtown Dallas, Texas.

He was shot with a rifle from a sixth-floor window, apparently by a lone gunman, former U.S. Marine Lee Harvey Oswald. Oswald was arrested within 40 minutes, but was himself shot and killed by local nightclub owner Jack Ruby two days later while being transferred to Dallas County Jail.

Since Kennedy's death there have been many conspiracy theories surrounding the assassination, with most Americans refusing to believe that Oswald acted alone. The events of that day remain a defining moment in 20th-century history, and spawned some incredible facts of their own.

MOVIE CAMERA▶ Dallas clothing manufacturer Abraham Zapruder captured the J.F.K. assassination on his home movie camera. He had arrived at the office that morning without it, and his secretary, Lillian Rogers, persuaded him to go home and fetch the camera, saying: "How many times will you have a crack at color movies of the President?" The Zapruder Film, as it became known, was sold two days later to *Life* magazine for $150,000—the equivalent of more than $1 million in today's money.

PINK SUIT▶ The pink suit that Jackie Kennedy wore on the day of the assassination is stored in a secret vault in the National Archives and Records Administration's complex in Maryland, where the temperature is kept at between 65 and 68°F (18 and 20°C), the humidity is 40 percent, and the air is changed six times an hour. The blood-splattered suit has never been cleaned, and only a handful of people have been allowed to see it since 1963.

LATE NEWS▶ Within 30 minutes of J.F.K.'s shooting, TV and radio reports relayed the news to more than 75 million Americans—but 12 jurors in a murder trial in Milwaukee, Wisconsin, did not hear about it until the evening of November 23. They had spent four days behind locked doors, and it was only when they reached their verdict on the Saturday night that the judge told them about Kennedy's assassination.

GRIEVING LETTERS▶ J.F.K.'s widow Jackie received more than 1.5 million condolence letters following her husband's assassination, 45,000 arriving at the White House on one day alone. Around 200,000 pages of letters were subsequently stored at the John F. Kennedy Library in Boston, Massachusetts, where they filled 170 ft (52 m) of shelf space.

COVER-UP?▶ A 2009 opinion poll found that only 10 percent of Americans believe that Lee Harvey Oswald acted alone in killing J.F.K. Seventy-four percent believe there was an official cover-up to keep the truth about the President's killing from the public.

FINAL FILM▸ In his final movie before entering politics, future U.S. President Ronald Reagan was filming *The Killers* with Lee Marvin and Angie Dickinson at Universal City in California when production was halted because of J.F.K.'s assassination. As President, Reagan himself survived an assassination attempt in 1981—the first sitting President to survive being shot by a would-be assassin.

CASKET RESTING PLACE▸ The casket that contained Kennedy's body on the flight to Washington, D.C., in preparation for his burial was later weighted and dropped by a U.S. Air Force plane into the Atlantic Ocean in an area where the disposal of test weapons left the seabed littered with munitions, making it too dangerous for anyone to try to recover it.

CHILD SUPPORT▸ After President Kennedy was killed, 11-year-old Jane Dryden from Austin, Texas, was so upset that she sent one condolence letter a week to the White House for the next six months.

KENNEDY MUSEUM▸ Located in the former Texas School Book Depository building from which Oswald fired the fatal shot, the Sixth Floor Museum in Dallas contains over 40,000 items relating to Kennedy's assassination.

HAT AUCTION▸ The gray fedora hat worn by Jack Ruby when he shot Lee Harvey Oswald was sold at auction in 2009 to an anonymous buyer for $53,775.

CONSPIRACY THEORIES▸ Numerous conspiracy theories surround J.F.K.'s assassination, alleged culprits including the C.I.A., the Cubans, the Russians, Vice President Lyndon Johnson, and U.S. mobsters. One theory even suggested that Kennedy was killed by an accidental discharge from the rifle of a Secret Service agent traveling in the car behind the President's limousine.

FOUR DEATHS▸ West Virginian Perry Gum's life spanned the deaths of all four assassinated U.S. presidents. He celebrated his 99th birthday on the day Kennedy was shot, and wrote in his letter to the White House that he had also lived through the assassinations of Abraham Lincoln (1865), James Garfield (1881), and William McKinley (1901).

KENNEDY AND LINCOLN

A series of spooky coincidences link the assassination of President Kennedy with that of President Abraham Lincoln almost 100 years earlier.

- **Lincoln was elected to Congress in 1846, Kennedy in 1946.**
- **Lincoln was elected as President in 1860, Kennedy in 1960.**
- **Both were assassinated on Fridays in front of their wives.**
- **Lincoln was shot in Ford's Theatre; Kennedy was shot in a Lincoln, made by Ford.**
- **Both Presidents' wives lost a child while living in the White House.**
- **Both assassins, John Wilkes Booth and Lee Harvey Oswald, were killed before facing trial.**
- **The surnames of both Presidents have seven letters.**
- **The names of both assassins have 15 letters.**
- **Their successors as President were both named Johnson.**
- **Andrew Johnson was born in 1808, Lyndon Johnson in 1908.**
- **Both assassinated Presidents were shot in the head.**
- **Both Presidents were particularly concerned with civil rights.**

Among the J.F.K. related exhibits in the Ripley collection is a lock of Lee Harvey Oswald's hair and his body identification (toe) tag. Ripley's also own the car in which Oswald traveled on the way to assassinate Kennedy.

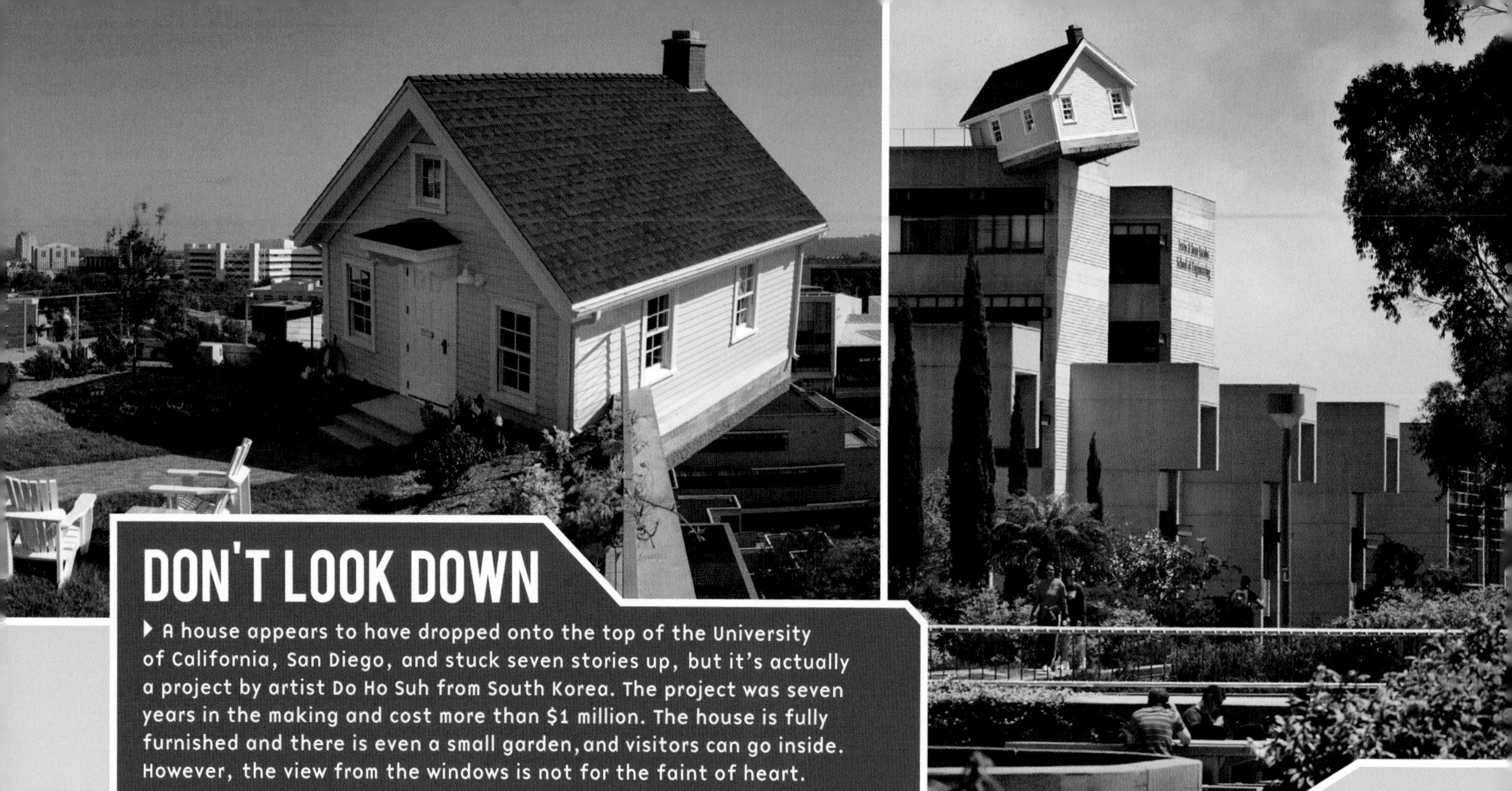

DON'T LOOK DOWN

▸ A house appears to have dropped onto the top of the University of California, San Diego, and stuck seven stories up, but it's actually a project by artist Do Ho Suh from South Korea. The project was seven years in the making and cost more than $1 million. The house is fully furnished and there is even a small garden, and visitors can go inside. However, the view from the windows is not for the faint of heart.

PEDAL POWER▸ Guests at the Cottage Lodge bed-and-breakfast hotel in Brockenhurst, England, can keep fit and help the environment by watching a bicycle-powered LCD TV in their room. To generate electricity for the set to operate, guests hop on the bike and pedal the power into the TV's battery pack.

POLAR RUN▸ Amundsen-Scott South Pole Station is home to the "300 Club," where participants warm up in a 200°F (93°C) sauna, then go out into –100°F (–73°C) or colder weather and run around the ceremonial South Pole—naked except for a pair of boots!

TIMBERRR!

▸ This incredible photograph shows lumberjacks working in the redwood forests of Humboldt, California, in the early 19th-century. Before the days of chainsaws and heavy machinery, giant trees were felled with axes and handsaws, and it could take a team of men a whole week to bring down one redwood, the largest trees in the world. The work was as risky as it looks, and even today, logging is one of the most dangerous occupations in the world.

10,000-YEAR CLOCK▸ Amazon.com founder Jeff Bezos is funding the $42-million construction of "The Clock of the Long Now," which is being built 500 ft (152 m) deep inside a Texas mountain, and is designed to keep time for 10,000 years. The clock will be 200 ft (60 m) tall, have a 5-ton pendulum, and will chime a different melody every day.

TOWERING CITY▸ Hong Kong is the skyscraper capital of the world. Its soaring skyline boasts more than 2,300 buildings at least 330 ft (100 m) tall—three times more than New York City.

RUSSIAN PRESENCE▸ The Norwegian island of Svalbard, which lies halfway between Norway and the North Pole, is home to only 2,000 people—yet it has its own Russian consulate.

WRONG PLACE▸ Chris and Frances Huntingford have been ordered to demolish their $375,000 four-bedroom dream home in Suffolk, England, because they built it 15 ft (4.5 m) to the right of where it should be.

WALL COLLAPSE▸ A 100-ft-long (30-m) section of the Great Wall of China in Zhangjiakou collapsed in 2012 after weeks of torrential rain—coupled with building work directly in front of the wall's foundations—that caused tons of bricks and rubble to crumble.

HIDDEN VOLCANOES▸ British surveyors have discovered a chain of 12 previously unknown undersea volcanoes off the coast of Antarctica, with a few coming within just 225 ft (70 m) of the surface.

UNDERWORLD

▸ Skarphedinn Thrainsson and Örvar Atli Porgeirsson explored the strange blue world under Europe's largest glacier, Vatnajökull, in Iceland, to capture on film the bizarre yet beautiful ice caves that lie hidden beneath. Air is squeezed out of the ancient ice in the glacier as it travels, making it a bright, clear, blue color. Venturing into these caves is a risky business, not just because of temperatures dropping to 10°F (–12°C) but because of the shifting ice, which has previously claimed the life of a photographer.

UGLY CONTEST

Contestants in the Concurso de Feos in Bilbao, Spain, twist and distort their eyes and mouth into hideous poses in a bid to scare—and impress—the judges as to who can make the ugliest face. The ugly competition is part of the nine-day Aste Nagusia festivity, which also includes music, circuses, bullfights, and fireworks.

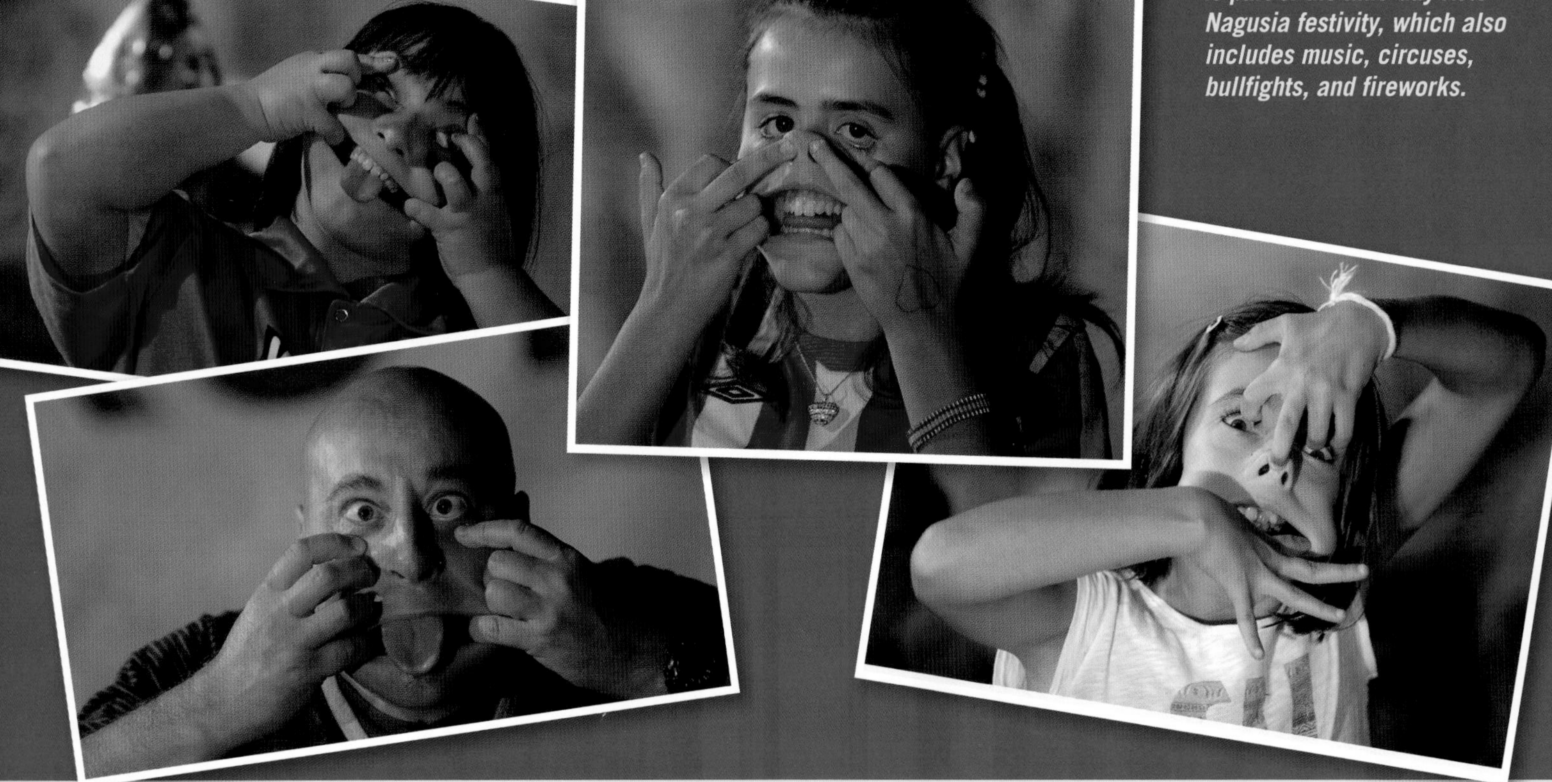

The Best Team
Sfera Race

BURIED ALIVE

▸ *Peter Skyllberg, 44, survived two months in a frozen car. He was found emaciated but alive in a car that had been buried in snow in northern Sweden for two months of a harsh winter. The car became stuck in drifts north of the town of Umea on December 19, 2011, and Peter wasn't rescued until February 17, 2012. He had survived on a few snacks and handfuls of snow, in temperatures that dropped to –22°F (–30°C). Some experts believe his body must have gone into a kind of human hibernation in order to survive the ordeal.*

BRIDGE STOLEN▶ Thieves in Slavkov, Czech Republic, escaped with a valuable haul of scrap metal after dismantling an 11-ton bridge and more than 650 ft (198 m) of railroad track.

TEDDY BEARS' PICNIC▶ A Finnish company offers people the chance to send their teddy bears on a trip to the Arctic Circle. For around $130, Teddy Tours Lapland poses the stuffed toys on horseback safari rides, taking walks in the snow, and, of course, enjoying picnics.

BOTTLED MESSAGES▶ Since 1996, Harold Hackett of Prince Edward Island, Canada, has tossed more than 5,000 bottled messages into the Atlantic Ocean—and has had about 3,300 people write back from as far afield as Russia, the Netherlands, Africa, and South America.

BATMAN STOPPED▶ Dressed as Batman, Lenny B. Robinson was driving his black Lamborghini "Batmobile" to surprise sick children in a hospital in Silver Spring, Maryland, when he was pulled over by police officers for having the wrong license plates on the car.

TOOTHBRUSH REPLACED▶ Astronauts Sunita Williams and Aki Hoshide carried out urgent repairs to the $100-billion International Space Station with a $3 toothbrush. By attaching the toothbrush to a metal pole, they were able to clean a troublesome bolt socket so that a malfunctioning power unit could be replaced.

CORPSE COOKS▶ Six days after she was pronounced dead and the day before her funeral, 95-year-old Li Xiufeng of Guangxi Province, China, stunned villagers by pushing open the lid of her coffin, climbing out, and cooking herself dinner.

RED FACES▶ Embarrassed parents realized that they had left their three-year-old daughter behind at a restaurant in Bel Air, Maryland, only when they saw her picture on the television news three hours later.

SILENT TREATMENT▶ A team of 120 mime artists was hired to control the traffic in Caracas, Venezuela. The initiative, dreamed up by the city's mayor, Carlos Ocariz, saw the mimes taking to the streets wearing clown costumes and wagging their fingers at any driver who violated traffic laws.

CONVERTED SHED▶ John Plumridge of Shropshire, England, spent more than four years converting his garden shed into a working pub that also displays a collection of 600 real ale and cider bottles. John's efforts resulted in first prize in a 2012 Shed of the Year competition.

LITTLE HOUDINI▶ Nicknamed "Little Houdini," Christopher Gay of Pleasant View, Tennessee, has escaped police custody 13 times—without resorting to any form of violence.

MINIATURE DIG▶ Since 2005, Joe Murray has been digging out the basement of his house in Saskatchewan, Canada, using only radio-controlled scale-model construction equipment. Working with his little tractors, excavators, and a miniature rock crusher, he has been able to move an average of just 9 cubic ft (0.25 cubic m) of earth each year.

SILVER HOARD▶ In March 2012, workers in St. Petersburg, Russia, discovered more than 1,000 pieces of jewelry and silver that had been hidden behind a wall since the 1917 Bolshevik Revolution.

LATE MAIL▶ A postcard mailed in 1943 from Rockford, Illinois, to sisters Pauline and Theresa Leisenring finally arrived at their former home in Elmira, New York, in 2012—69 years after it was sent and more than 50 years after both women had died.

GIANT ORANGES▶ Sharon Cole of Modesto, California, noticed these very large oranges growing on a tree in her garden. The largest measures a whopping 24 in (61 cm) in circumference.

WITCH WORSHIP▸ The U.S. military has built an $80,000 Stonehenge-like stone circle at its Air Force Academy in Colorado so that cadets, including druids, pagans, Wiccans, and witches, who practice "Earth-based" religions have somewhere to worship.

MIDDLE AMERICA▸ The town of Kinsley, Kansas, has a road sign pointing to San Francisco, California, on the west coast and New York City on the east, with a distance of 1,561 mi (2,512 km) to each one.

DEADLY SEA▸ Although the Dead Sea's high salt content allows a person to float effortlessly on the surface, drownings there are common. It is Israel's second most dangerous swimming area.

FAMILY HOME▸ Berkeley Castle in Gloucestershire, England, has been home to the Berkeley family for 900 continuous years. The current heir, Charles Berkeley, will be the 27th generation of the family to live there.

KETTLE DRUMS WERE ONCE USED AS CURRENCY ON ALOR ISLAND, INDONESIA.

TIME FLIES!▸ At the end of 2011, Samoa changed its time zone to the west side of the International Date Line, making it possible to celebrate a single holiday two days in a row by flying 30 minutes east to American Samoa, which opted to stay east of the Date Line.

DRIFTING DOCK▸ A 66-ft-long (20-m) concrete and metal dock that was carried away from Japan by the 2011 tsunami washed ashore on a beach near Newport, Oregon, in June 2012. It was identified via a commemorative plaque and by the discovery of a starfish native to Japan that was still clinging to the structure 15 months after it went adrift. In total, more than 1.5 million tons of tsunami debris drifted across the Pacific toward the west coast of North America.

STREET EELS▸ Dozens of slimy eels were found in puddles and gutters in the flooded streets of Masterton, New Zealand, in March 2012 following heavy rain and storms. The eels came from nearby sewerage ponds that had overflowed with the torrential rain.

WOMAN'S WORLD▸ In the Indian state of Meghalaya, people live in a matrilineal culture—where property and wealth pass to daughters rather than to sons, and children take the mother's surname.

CLIFF CORRIDOR

▸ Until 40 years ago, the only way to reach Guoliang village in Henan Province, China, was via 720 steep steps—but then 14 villagers joined forces to build a precarious 4,100-ft-long (1,250-m) road tunnel perched 360 ft (110 m) up on a cliff face. With no electricity or heavy machinery, they used their hands to chisel and hammer the 16-ft-high (5-m), 13-ft-wide (4-m) cliff corridor out of the mountainside over a five-year period, during which they went through 10 tons of drill rods and 4,000 hammers.

CHURCH PERCH▸ The 130-ft-tall (40-m) Katskhi Pillar near Chiatura, Georgia, has an orthodox monastery perched on top that dates back more than 1,200 years. Its inaccessibility meant that the monastery stood deserted for 700 years, but visitors can now reach it by climbing an iron ladder that extends all the way from the ground to the summit.

HIGH SCHOOL▸ To reach their school in Pili in China's mountainous Xinjiang Uygur region, some 40 pupils, guided by parents and teachers, must carefully pick their way along a narrow rocky pass located 1,500 ft (457 m) above a sheer drop.

SINKING CITY▸ The Italian city of Venice has been sinking into the water and tilting east into the Adriatic Sea by 0.08 in (2 mm) per year over the last decade—five times quicker than previously thought.

SHOW AND SMELL▸ Sweden's Lund University displays a collection of more than 100 plaster casts of noses belonging to notable Scandinavians, including a cast of the false silver-and-gold nose of Danish astronomer Tycho Brahe (1546–1601), who lost his original nose in a sword duel.

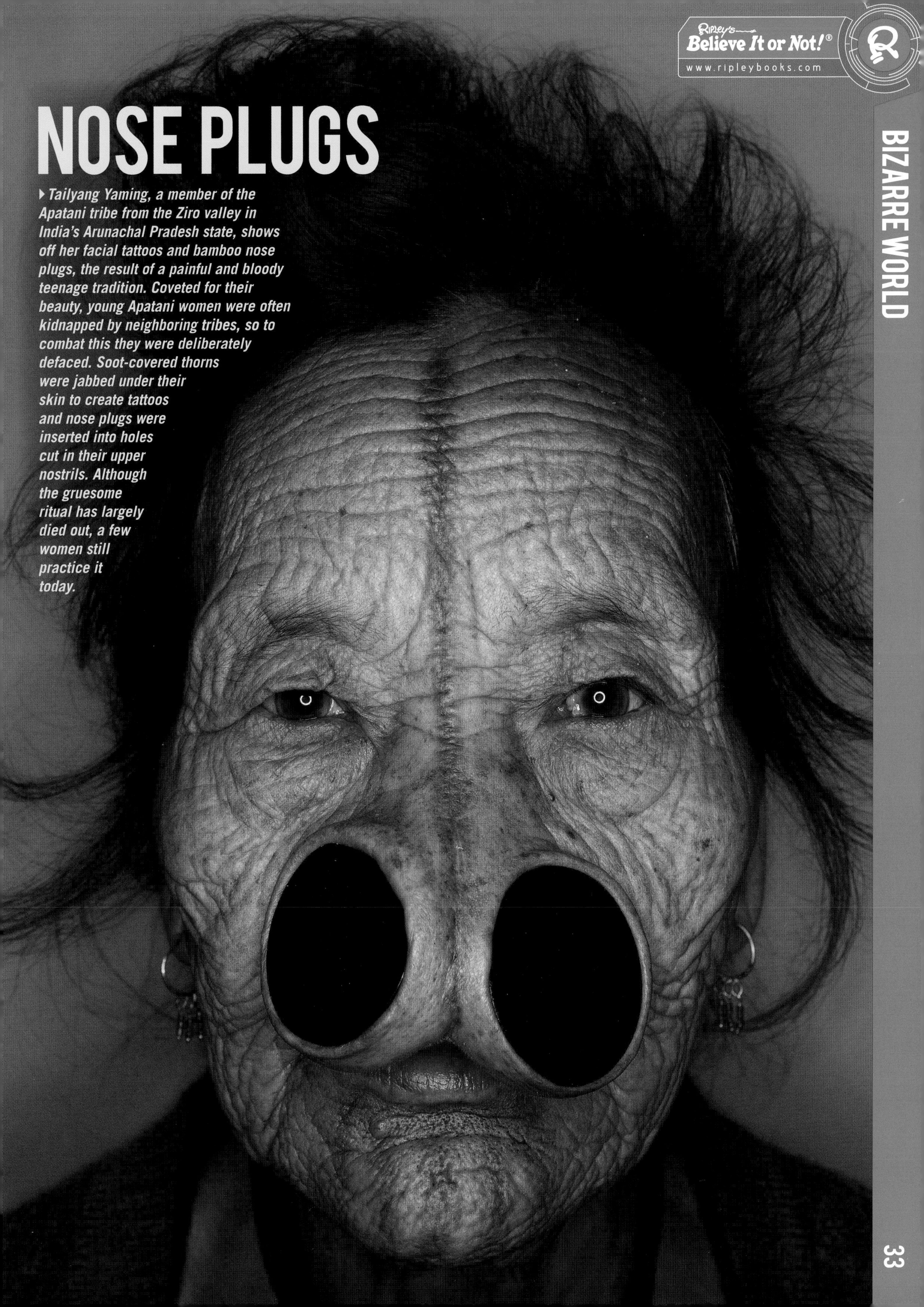

NOSE PLUGS

▸ *Tailyang Yaming, a member of the Apatani tribe from the Ziro valley in India's Arunachal Pradesh state, shows off her facial tattoos and bamboo nose plugs, the result of a painful and bloody teenage tradition. Coveted for their beauty, young Apatani women were often kidnapped by neighboring tribes, so to combat this they were deliberately defaced. Soot-covered thorns were jabbed under their skin to create tattoos and nose plugs were inserted into holes cut in their upper nostrils. Although the gruesome ritual has largely died out, a few women still practice it today.*

INDEX

Page numbers in italic refer to the illustrations

A

airplane, ice falls from 8
algae, giant bloom of 16
Antarctica
  alkaline lake under ice 16
  sauna at South Pole 26
  snow at South Pole 16
  underwater volcanoes 26
apples, tornado causes avalanche of 10
Arctic, teddy bears visit 31
Aslett, Don (USA) 19

B

balls
  fall from sky 22
  long lost 16
  water tanks look like 9, *9*
bank, robbed by hypnosis 14
Batman 31
beach, beside sinkhole 11, *11*
bees, harvesting honey from cliff *20–21*, 21
Berkeley family (UK) 32
Bezos, Jeff (USA) 26
bicycle, in tree 14, *14*
birds, crash onto parking lots 11
books, giant mural of 19, *19*
Booth, John Wilkes (USA) 25
Boring, William (USA) 11
bottles
  houses made of 19
  messages in 31
Brahe, Tycho (Den) 32
bridges
  goats stranded on 10, *10*
  underwater 11
Burciaga, Sonia (Mex) 18

C

Campbell, Phil and Phyllis 16
cars
  Batman arrested 31
  drive-in church services 11
  man survives being buried in snow 30, *30*
  mime artists control traffic 31
  multiple traffic violations 22
castle, family lives in for long time 32
caves, in glacier 27, *27*
churches
  drive-in services 11
  made of snow 19
cities
  covered in clay 8
  sinking 32
cleaners, museum of 19
cliffs
  harvesting honey from *20–21*, 21
  tunnel cut through by hand 32, *32*
clock, enormous 26
clouds
  tubular 22
  weight of 22
Cole, Sharon (USA) 31, *31*
corpses
  air burial 14
  comes back to life 31
  exhumed 6–7, *6–7*
  holding hands 22
  as mannequin 18, *18*

D

Dead Sea, drowning risk in 32
divers, women 8
Do Ho Suh (Kor) 26, *26*
drainage, hall of fame 22
drums, as currency 32
Dryden, Jane (USA) 25
Dyball, Roger (UK) 14

E

Eakin, Thomas C. (USA) 14
earthquakes 8, 16
eels, flood washes into town 32
eggs, Russian Egg Roulette 19
elections
  on Tuesdays 10
  unopposed candidate 14
electricity
  bicycle-powered TV 26
  massive outage 19
Esparza, Pascuala (Mex) 18

F

face, competition for ugliest 28, *28–9*
Ferris wheel, man-powered 14
fire
  fire tornado 17, *17*
  fireball fight 9
  Yosemite firefall 8, *8*
fish, large number of species in lake 8
flies, restrictions on numbers in lavatories 14
floods, eels washed into town 32
flour, fighting with 11, 19
flowers, night-flowering 16
forest, buried by volcano 16

G

Garfield, James (USA) 24
Gay, Christopher (USA) 31
gel, falls from sky 16
glaciers
  caves in 27, *27*
  ice stolen from 11
goats, stranded on bridge 10, *10*
Great Wall of China 26
Gum, Perry (USA) 24
gym, aerobics cause tremor 14

H

Hackett, Harold (Can) 31
hail storm 16
Harms, Virgil (USA) 14
Higgins, Jim (UK) 8
honey, harvesting from cliff *20–21*, 21
Hong Kong, skyscrapers 26
Hoshide, Aki (Jap) 31
hotels
  bicycle-powered TV 26
  inflatable rooms 22
  knitted room 19
  in mine 10
houses
  basement excavated with models 31
  built round railway carriage 8
  demolition ordered 26
  made of bottles 19
  missile silo made into 11
  road built around 22, *22*
  in shape of snail 22
  on top of building 26, *26*
Huntingford, Chris and Frances (UK) 26
hypnosis, robbery by 14

I

ice
  caves in glacier 27, *27*
  falls through cathedral roof 8
  lake under 16
  stolen from glacier 11
International Space Station 31
island, with Russian consulate 26

J

Jenkins, Kate (UK) 19
jewelry, hoard found 31
Johnson, Andrew (USA) 25
Johnson, Lyndon (USA) 25

K

Kennedy, Jackie (USA) 24–25, *24–25*
Kennedy, John F. (USA) 24–25, *24–25*
knitting, in hotel room 19

L

lakes
  alkaline water 16
  disappearing 22
  large number of fish species in 8
  sphagnum moss island in 16
  turns red 19, *19*
languages
  polyglot island 16
  undiscovered 14
Larson, Dick (USA) 14, *14*
Leisenrig, Pauline and Theresa (USA) 31
Li Xiufeng (Chn) 31
lightbulb, burns continuously 14
lightning
  huge number of strikes 8
  male victims 10
  surviving multiple strikes 16
Lincoln, Abraham (USA) 24, 25
lipstick, damages tomb 16
Luo Baogen (Chn) 22, *22*

M

MacGinnis, Dr. John (UK) 14
McKinley, William (USA) 24
mail, long lost postcard 31
mannequin, corpse as 18, *18*
Menninger, Bonar (USA) 25
meteorite, town built on crash site 14
mime artists, control traffic 31
mine, hotel room in 10
Mize, Carl (USA) 16
molasses, toxic dump cleaned up with 16
monastery, inaccessible 32
money, drums as currency 32
motorcycles, washed up on beach 14
mountain, school on 32
mummies, exhumed 6–7, *6–7*
Murakami, Misaki (Jap) 16
mural, of book spines 19, *19*
Murray, Joe (Can) 31

N

names
  Boring and Dull towns 11
  children take mother's surname 32
New York, sunsets in Manhattan 16
nose
  large collection of plaster casts of 32
  nose plugs 33, *33*

O

Ocariz, Carlos (Ven) 31
Olympic Games 22
oranges, large 31, *31*
Oswald, Lee Harvey (USA) 24, 25, *25*